NOW YOU CAN READ....
Puss in Boots

STORY ADAPTED BY LUCY KINCAID

ILLUSTRATED BY ERIC KINCAID

BRIMAX BOOKS • CAMBRIDGE • ENGLAND

Once there was a miller who had three sons. When he died he left his eldest son the mill. He left his second eldest son the donkey. He had nothing to leave John, his youngest son, except the cat.

John's brothers laughed. "You will never make a fortune with a cat," they said.

"Master" said the cat when John and he were alone. "Buy me a pair of boots and I WILL make you a fortune." It was plain to see the cat was no ordinary cat.

John did as the
cat asked. He
bought him a pair
of boots. The
cat put them on.

"Now give me a
sack and I will
go hunting," said
Puss in Boots,
as he was to be
known from then
on.

Puss in Boots went
into the forest.
He caught a rabbit.
Instead of taking
it home to John
he took it to the
King's palace.
"I have a present
for the King," he
said.

"I am Puss in Boots," he said to the King. "I have brought you a present from my master, the Marquis of Carrabas."

"Thank you very much," said the King. Kings are like everyone else. They like getting presents.

Puss in Boots went hunting every day. Everything he caught he took to the King. Every day he said, "This is a present from my master the Marquis of Carrabas."

One day, the King said, "I would like to meet your master. I will call my coach. You can take me to see him."

"I cannot ride with you," said Puss in Boots. "I have some business to attend to. I will meet you at my master's castle."
"Very well!" said the King.

The Princess said she would ride with the King. They got into the coach and set off.

On the way they passed some men working in the fields. "Who owns this land?" called the King.
"The Marquis of Carrabas!" answered the men. Puss in Boots had already passed that way. HE had told the men what to say if the King spoke to them.

There were men cutting wood in the forest. "Who owns THIS land?" called the King.

"The Marquis of Carrabas!" replied the wood cutters. Puss in Boots had told THEM what to say too.

"The Marquis of Carrabas must be a very rich man," said the King.

When Puss in Boots got home he called to John. "Quick master! Go to the river and bathe."

"Why?" asked John.

"Just do as I say!" said Puss in Boots.

John was puzzled but he did as he was told. He was even more puzzled when Puss ran off with his clothes and hid them under a bush.

"Help! Help!" called Puss in Boots when he saw the King's coach coming. "Help! Help! My master, the Marquis of Carrabas, is drowning!"

"Someone has stolen my master's clothes," said Puss, when John was rescued.

The King lent John his cloak and invited him to ride in the royal coach.

"The Marquis of Carrabas is very handsome," thought the Princess.

"My master's castle is just over the next hill," said Puss in Boots. "I will run on ahead and prepare for your arrival."

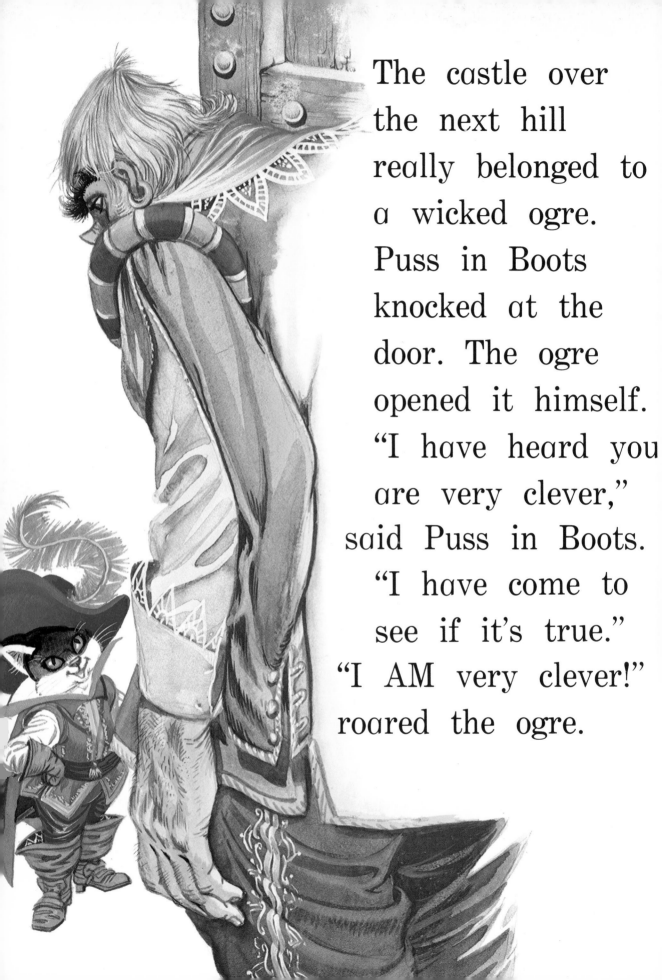

The castle over the next hill really belonged to a wicked ogre. Puss in Boots knocked at the door. The ogre opened it himself. "I have heard you are very clever," said Puss in Boots. "I have come to see if it's true." "I AM very clever!" roared the ogre.

"I can change myself into ANYTHING I please." The ogre snapped his fingers and changed himself into a lion. He growled at Puss in Boots. Puss pretended not to be afraid.

"It's EASY to change into something big," said Puss in Boots. "I don't suppose you can change yourself into something as small as . . . as small as a mouse!"

"OH, YES I CAN!" roared the ogre. AND HE DID. But before he could change back again Puss in Boots gobbled him up. And that was the end of the ogre.

"You have a new master now," said Puss in Boots to the people who lived in the castle. "He is the Marquis of Carrabas. The King is bringing him here now. We must prepare a feast."

"Hooray for the King!" they shouted.

"Hooray for the Marquis!"

"HOORAY FOR PUSS IN BOOTS!"

When the King's coach arrived Puss in Boots was waiting at the castle door.

"Welcome! Welcome to the castle of the Marquis of Carrabas," he said.

"Who IS this Marquis of Carrabas?" whispered John.

"YOU are!" said Puss in Boots.

"Am I?" said John. He was very surprised.

John married the Princess, and they lived in the castle. Many years later, they moved into the palace and John became King. Puss in Boots HAD made John's fortune for him, just as he said he would.

All these appear in the pages of the story. Can you find them?

cat

boots

sack

rabbit